ALEXANDER DUMAS'S

THE THREE MUSKETEERS

A GRAPHIC NOVEL

BY R. STAHLBERG
& EVA CABRERA

RAINTREE BOOKS
A CAPSTONE IMPRINT

Raintree is an imprint of Capstone Global Library
Limited, a company incorporated in England and Wales
having its registered office at 264 Banbury Road, Oxford,
OX2 7DY – Registered company number:6695582

www.raintree.co.uk
myorders@raintree.co.uk

Designer: Kyle Grenz

ISBN 978-1-4747-2607-8 (paperback)
20 19 18 17 16
10 9 8 7 6 5 4 3 2 1

British Library Cataloguing in Publication Data
A full catalogue record for this book is available from the
British Library.

Every effort has been made to contact copyright holders
of material reproduced in this book. Any omissions
will be rectified in subsequent printings if notice is given
to the publisher.

Printed and bound in China.

CONTENTS

ALL ABOUT *THE THREE MUSKETEERS*

Alexander Dumas's book *The Three Musketeers* is classified as historical fiction. The main plot and some of the characters are a result of Dumas's imagination, but there are some bits and pieces that are historically accurate.

For starters, the Musketeers did in fact exist in the 17th century, the time period in which the book is set. They were an elite part of the French army. During peacetime, they were the King's personal escort. Captain Treville did have control of the Musketeers. His quarrel with Cardinal Richelieu is also historically correct. As a result of this quarrel, the King was eventually forced to send Treville into exile. The King and Queen in the story were for the most part written accurately. To historians, they are known as King Louis XIII and Queen Anne.

Dumas takes his biggest leaps of fiction with his main characters. D'Artagnan in real life was named Charles de Batz-Castelmore. Like D'Artagnan, Charles de Batz-Castelmore served as a Musketeer. Eventually, he served as the Captain of the Musketeers. But the timeline and romances that Dumas created are false. D'Artagnan's friends, Porthos, Athos and Aramis, are also based on real people. Porthos is based on Isaac de Partau. Aramis is Henry d'Aramitz, and Athos is Armand de Sillegne. All three were Musketeers in real life, but little else is known about their lives.

The one main character that Dumas created mainly from fiction was Milady, or the Lady de Winter. Dumas's villainess was historically an exiled lady-in-waiting to Queen Anne. In real life, Milady did none of the cruel acts that Dumas wrote she did.

Whatever Dumas's reasons for exaggeration, the events in the story make a compelling read. The blend of fact and fiction is in part what makes *The Three Musketeers* such a great novel.

COUNT DE ROCHEFORT

THE DUKE OF BUCKINGHAM

ATHOS

ARAMIS

PORTHOS

CAPTAIN TREVILLE

MILADY (LADY DE WINTER)

CARDINAL RICHELIEU

KING LOUIS XIII

QUEEN ANNE OF AUSTRIA

D'ARTAGNAN

CONSTANCE BONACIEUX

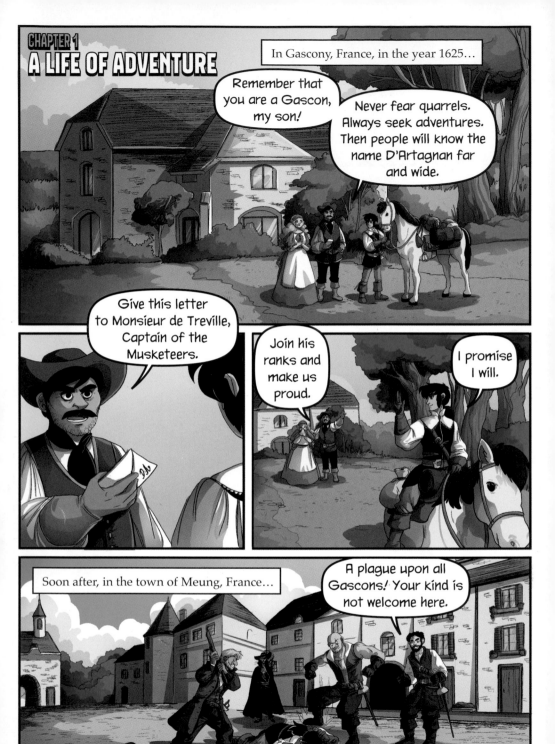

Much later, outside a residence in Paris…

You walked here all the way from Meung?!

Yes, Monsieur Bonacieux. A man from Meung stole my money, so I had to sell my horse.

May I rent one of your apartments?

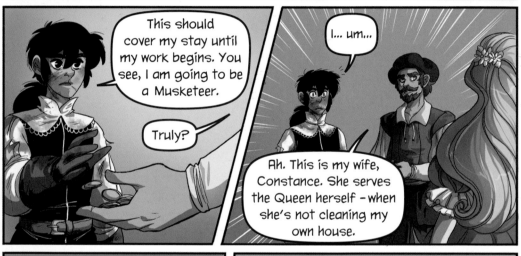

This should cover my stay until my work begins. You see, I am going to be a Musketeer.

Truly?

I… um…

Ah. This is my wife, Constance. She serves the Queen herself – when she's not cleaning my own house.

Shall she prepare your room, good sir?

I would be honoured.

After buying new clothes and a sword, D'Artagnan visits the Musketeers' meeting hall.

Wait here. I'll let Captain Treville know you're here.

Finish the story, Porthos.

The story is that the Cardinal ordered Rochefort to spy upon the man ...

... and then cut his throat for treason!

That certainly sounds like the Cardinal. Or the Red Duke, as I like to call him.

Ha! It's too bad you didn't follow your first vocation, Aramis.

You would've made an impressive priest.

Surely these fellows will all be imprisoned or hanged for such scandalous talk. I'd best avoid them, for my own safety.

HA HA HA HAHA

Sir, before we three could even draw our swords, two of our allies were killed.

We were lucky to escape alive.

I will not allow fighting in the streets! Above all, I will not let you three give the Cardinal's guards a reason to laugh at us!

I ... did not know that.

But still – you must not risk your lives opposing the Cardinal. Brave men like you are hard to replace.

Now get Athos to a surgeon. Clearly he's been wounded.

Begone.

Now what can I do for you, son? Quickly now, my time is limited.

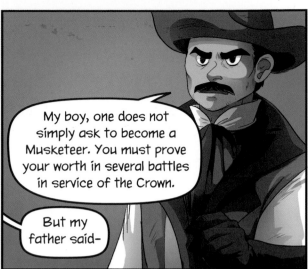

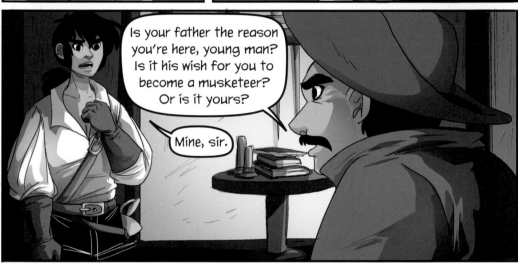

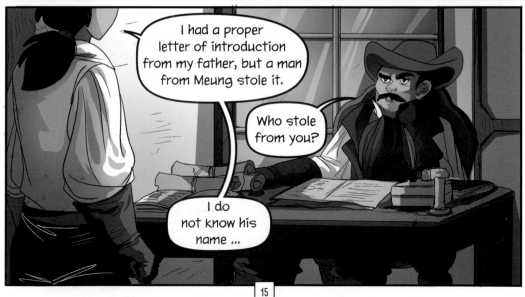

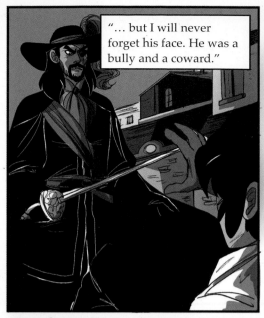

CHAPTER 2

FRIENDS AND ENEMIES

He will not escape me this time!

Back from the doctor so soon, Athos?

I told you it's nothing serious.

Ow!

THUMP

Excuse me – I'm in a hurry!

Excuse me? Think again, boy!

M-Monsieur Athos? Please forgive me–

It's too late for apologies, Monsieur Man-in-a-Hurry.

After several hours of fruitless searching...

Curse my pride. If I survive these duels alive, I must practise being more polite.

Monsieur, I believe you dropped your handkerchief. You'd be sorry to lose such a fine item.

Allow me—

MdBT?

Oh, dear Aramis! Try to tell us now that you're not in love with Madame de Bois-Tracy.

Sigh ... I suppose we duel at two o'clock, then. You name the place.

Noon that very day...

My death may be certain, but I will not go quietly.

Oh, so now you wish to show me respect.

I did not mean to–

Spare me.

I have asked two friends to witness our duel, but they have not yet arrived.

We do not need to do this now, Athos.

You are wounded and would be at a disadvantage.

SCHING

I fight with either hand just as easily.

What's this I see?

The next day, at King Louis's royal castle...

Captain Treville! Cardinal Richilieu says that your Musketeers are criminals. He wants them hanged.

No, your Highness. My men's swords serve only your Majesty. They were forced to defend themselves.

I humbly request that your Majesty have Cardinal Richilieu explain why his guards were arresting my men.

You have a point. With that said, duels are forbidden. They must be punished.

Respectfully, your highness, one of my three men was already wounded.

The fourth is just a boy. Were it my decision alone, such bravery would not be punished.

It would be rewarded.

Hmm...

Later, at a local pub…

I've never held so much money in my life! What should I do with it?

Double it at the gambling tables.

Hire a servant.

If I were you, I'd find a girlfriend and spend it on her.

Truly, Aramis? I thought you planned to become a priest.

Until I take those vows, I intend to enjoy life to the fullest.

As do we all. From this day forth, you are one of us, D'Artagnan.

Stand. Speak the oath with us.

ALL FOR ONE... ...ONE FOR ALL!

CHAPTER 3
DANGEROUS LIAISONS

D'Artagnan excels in his training at the academy. In a short time, he graduates at the head of his class and is hired as a Royal Guard.

Soon after…

Morbleu, What is the meaning of this?

The Cardinal demands to speak with you.

What would Cardinal Richelieu want with my landlord?

Has your wife shared any royal secrets with you?

What? No. She barely speaks to me these days.

You four, wait here for Madame Bonacieux to return.

I cannot allow Constance to be taken!

Please forgive me – and be on your way.

But be careful.

I take it back – you are a gentleman after all.

But D'Artagnan could not leave her sight. He was in love – and worried for Constance's safety…

That man looks like trouble!

D'Artagnan?

I'm sorry, Madame, but you are not safe. I need to know your business.

You need to know nothing, Monsieur!

I have only devotion and sympathy in my heart. Can't you see that?

What is the matter here?

Lord Duke of Buckingham?!

If you are offering to help us, then I accept.

Follow me at a discreet distance. If you see anyone following us, stop them.

On my honour.

Fortunately, they soon arrived at the Louvre without a fight.

Once there, Constance led the Duke to a secret chamber...

Anne, my love!

Oh, my dear duke, you risk both your life and my honour by seeing me in secret like this.

I only want what you want – for us to be together.

Meanwhile...

Take this fool away.

Please let me go! I've told you everything I know!

And I thank you for that, M'sieur Bonacieux.

Report.

The Queen and Duke have seen each other, Cardinal. Late last night.

Why am I only hearing of this now?

My spy in the Louvre was detained. I'm sorry.

How can we reveal the Queen's affair now? The point of luring the Duke here to Paris was to have witnesses of their secret meeting.

My spy also believes the Duke left the meeting with a rosewood casket with diamonds inside.

Well then, Rochefort – all is not lost. Now listen carefully and do exactly as I say...

Do you see now? I am betrayed on all sides.

No, for I am on your side. Please let me help.

Later, at the Bonacieux house...

My husband! You're home.

What's left of it, anyway. Did you stop cleaning while I was being tortured?

I beg for your forgiveness.

I've had grave matters to deal with.

Graver than my imprisonment?

Yes, I'm afraid so. It is a good and holy act. And there is money to be gained...

Yes. Will you deliver this for me? You must not be seen.

Money, you say?

D'Artagnan, Athos, Porthos and Aramis rode out together under cover of darkness.

The Cardinal's spies were everywhere.

AMBUSH!

BANG

BANG

Escape, D'Artagnan! We'll cover you.

BANG

I will not abandon you.

Your mission will fail if you die here.

Reluctantly, D'Artagnan left the three Musketeers behind. He raced to Calais, on the northern coast.

Upon arrival...

D'Artagnan travelled to England without problems.

Monsieur Duke!

Stand down. I know this man.

Why have you gone to such lengths to see me in person, young man?

Our mutual friend is in great danger. Only you, your Grace, can save her.

What's happened?

Read this.

God in Heaven!

Follow me, young man.

Upon D'Artagnan's return...

I am so happy to find you all alive and well.

Pah! It takes more than a few of the Cardinal's spies to defeat us.

Enough chit-chat.

Agreed. What happened in London, D'Artagnan?

Thankfully, the Lady de Winter only stole two of the diamonds.

She only needed two to prove the Duke and the Queen were having an affair.

Indeed. So, the Duke hired jewellers to create exact copies of the missing studs ...

"... After the studs were finished, I hurried to the King's Ball."

Sire, here is the proof. The proof that your Queen has been having an affair.

France owes you a great debt, young man. As do I.

It is an honour to serve France and you, madame. I ask for nothing more.

How noble. All the same, please accept this ring as my thanks.

Someone else wishes to thank you as well.

Constance!

You sure know how to tell a tale, D'Artagnan.

It's all true, Monseiur. On my honour.

Oh, I believe you. But not a word of it can leave this room.

But the Cardinal is a criminal! He needs—

He needs to be watched carefully. I will handle that ...

... You four have other work to do. The siege of La Rochelle has resumed.

The last trading port open to England is under attack? This must be the Cardinal's doing.

So soon after his plan to destroy the Queen failed?

I agree. He's trying to start a war.

His motives don't matter. Stopping the siege is our priority.

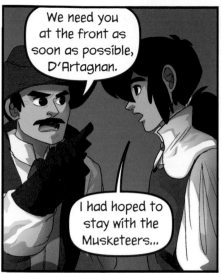

CHAPTER 4
MILADY'S REVENGE

Something is wrong. I feel it in my bones.

Is that a—

BANG

"Special" mission indeed.

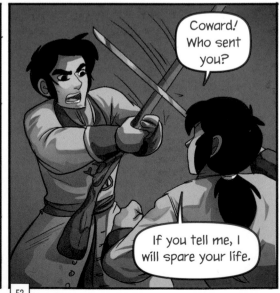

Coward! Who sent you?

If you tell me, I will spare your life.

Some days later…

D'Artagnan! A gift has arrived for you. It's from Paris.

A dozen bottles of wine? From Athos, Porthos and Aramis!

I shall drink to their health.

But I will not drink alone. We shall celebrate, friends!

That night...

And now for the moment you've all been waiting for.

Hear, hear!

In a nearby, quiet place...

Tell us everything you know about this "Milady."

I've never met her. But it's clear she holds a deep grudge against me, though.

Well, we think we've discovered her identity.

How? Tell me who wants me dead!

It was a simple matter ...

"... we listened to her conversation through a chimney."

I stole your diamonds. YOUR mistake ruined the plan – not mine.

I have a back-up plan. I simply need you to get close to the Duke again.

Very well. I will kill the Duke for you. But you must kill someone for me in exchange.

Surely D'Artagnan is dead by now.

He is not enough.

Find Constance Bonacieux. Kill her along with her husband.

That is easily done.

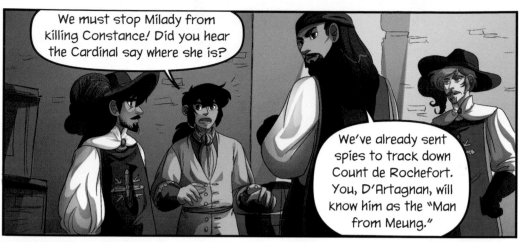

We must stop Milady from killing Constance! Did you hear the Cardinal say where she is?

We've already sent spies to track down Count de Rochefort. You, D'Artagnan, will know him as the "Man from Meung."

"Where Rochefort goes, Milady will follow."

ROCHEFORT!!

Remember me?

This is not the way that I wished to avenge myself, but we do what we can.

Stay here, Madame.

What is happening out there? Did I hear gunfire?

Yes?

Oh, dear me! I must speak with Constance Bonacieux at once.

D'Artagnan sent me.

Constance! The Cardinal has found you! We must leave here while D'Artagnan holds them back.

D'Artagnan is here?!

There's no time to explain. You must come with me.

O-okay.

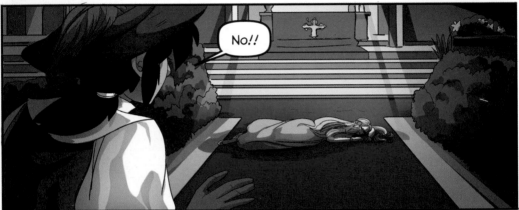

Not long after, back at the siege camp…

What is the meaning of this? Release Count de Rochefort.

We will speak with the Cardinal. Now.

Stand down. Let them in – after they release Rochefort.

You know I can have you arrested.

You abandoned your posts. You attacked my guards. You abducted one of my men.

This man was acting on your orders to murder the Queen's maid, Constance Bonacieux.

I see. Then how much money do you want?

That is why you're here, no? You haven't arrested me, so clearly you wish me to buy your silence.

For now, we only want one thing ...

"... Tell us the whereabouts of Lady de Winter –"

"– The one they call 'Milady.'"

"And grant us a warrant for her arrest."

Go on, then. Kill me. That's why you're here, isn't it?

No, Milady. In the name of the King, I place you under arrest.

You will pay for your crimes.

D'Artagnan served in the King's army during the siege with distinction.

After the siege ended, D'Artagnan was officially made a Musketeer. The other Musketeers made sure that the Cardinal himself wrote a letter of recommendation for him.

Congratulations, my boy.

But be careful. You've made a powerful enemy.

What's this, Cardinal Richilieu?

Read it. Fill in the name of whomever you like.

This makes us even.

What is it?

This is a commission for the rank of First Lieutenant. Each of you deserves this far more than I do.

ALL FOR ONE... ...ONE FOR ALL!

ABOUT THE RETELLING AUTHOR AND ILLUSTRATOR

L. R. Stahlberg has been part of the comic book industry for the better part of two decades, as a small press writer, an indie self-publisher and a distributor of comics and games. His debut in the young adult comic market was writing an adaptation of *Moby Dick*. He's also been part of the New Pulp movement with novellas in the crime, spy thriller, superhero and supernatural genres. He was nominated in 2014 by the New Pulp Awards for Best New Writer.

Eva Cabrera is a sequential artist born in Jalapa, Veracruz, Mexico. She is currently the art director of Neggi Studio and an illustrator at Zombie Studio. She also illustrates comic books for Protobunker Studio as the main artist for *El Arsenal: Been Caught Stealing*. She has won several comic-related national contests and has participated in various art expos. In her spare time, Eva feeds her addiction to coffee and the internet.

GLOSSARY

baldric belt for a cloak, worn over from one shoulder and across the opposite hip

devotion time, effort or attention given to some purpose

discreet showing good judgement in not attracting attention

endure put up with something unpleasant or painful

enmity big, unfriendly feeling

insolent insulting and outspoken

oppose against something and try to prevent it from happening

plague something that troubles and annoys you

quarrel argument

reinforcement extra troops sent to strengthen a fighting force

sanctity being holy, very important or valuable

scandalous dishonest or immoral act that shocks people and disgraces those involved

sheathe put something, such as a sword, into its holder

siege surrounding of a place to cut off supplies and then wait for those inside to surrender

COMPREHENSION QUESTIONS
READING QUESTIONS

1. D'Artagnan becomes friends with Porthos, Athos and Aramis after almost dueling all three of them. Have you ever made a friend when you weren't expecting to? What happened?

2. "All for one, one for all!" is the motto of the Musketeers. How do D'Artagnan and the three Musketeers follow this motto throughout the book?

3. Captain Treville tells D'Artagnan that he has to prove himself before he can become a Musketeer. Why do you think D'Artagnan must do this?

COMPREHENSION QUESTIONS
WRITING PROMPTS

1. Pretend you are D'Artagnan's father. Write the letter of introduction that D'Artagnan was supposed to give to Monsieur de Treville.

2. Imagine that you are a Musketeer. Write a journal entry about your day-to-day activities.

3. Write a new ending! What would've happened if D'Artagnan had made it to Constance before Milady found her?

READ THEM ALL!

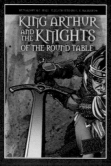

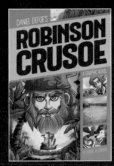

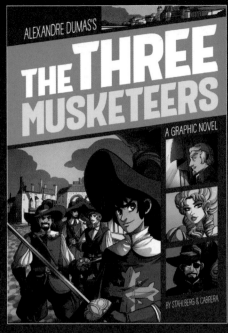

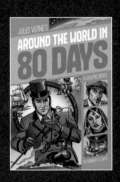

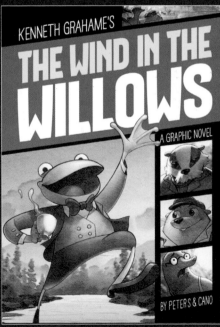

ONLY FROM RAINTREE BOOKS!